T0368454

"The Talking Bug"
The Bug that talks Back

La'Tanya Y'vette Patty

AuthorHouse™
1663 Liberty Drive
Bloomington, IN 47403
www.authorhouse.com
Phone: 833-262-8899

Because of the dynamic nature of the Internet, any web addresses or links contained
in this book may have changed since publication and may no longer be valid. The views
expressed in this work are solely those of the author and do not necessarily reflect the views
of the publisher, and the publisher hereby disclaims any responsibility for them.

Any people depicted in stock imagery provided by Getty Images are models,
and such images are being used for illustrative purposes only.
Certain stock imagery © Getty Images.

This book is printed on acid-free paper.

ISBN: 979-8-8230-3346-6 (sc)
ISBN: 979-8-8230-3347-3 (e)

Library of Congress Control Number: 2024918745

Print information available on the last page.

Published by AuthorHouse 01/22/2025

authorHOUSE®

"The Talking Bug"

The Bug that talks Back

"What are you doing in here? "You, Sonamabiscuit" I told you, don't come in my house. I am sick and tired of you. OK, you are running. When I catch you, I am going to flush you down the toilet, said the lady"

"Please don't. There is a lot of water down there, and I can't swim," said the bug.

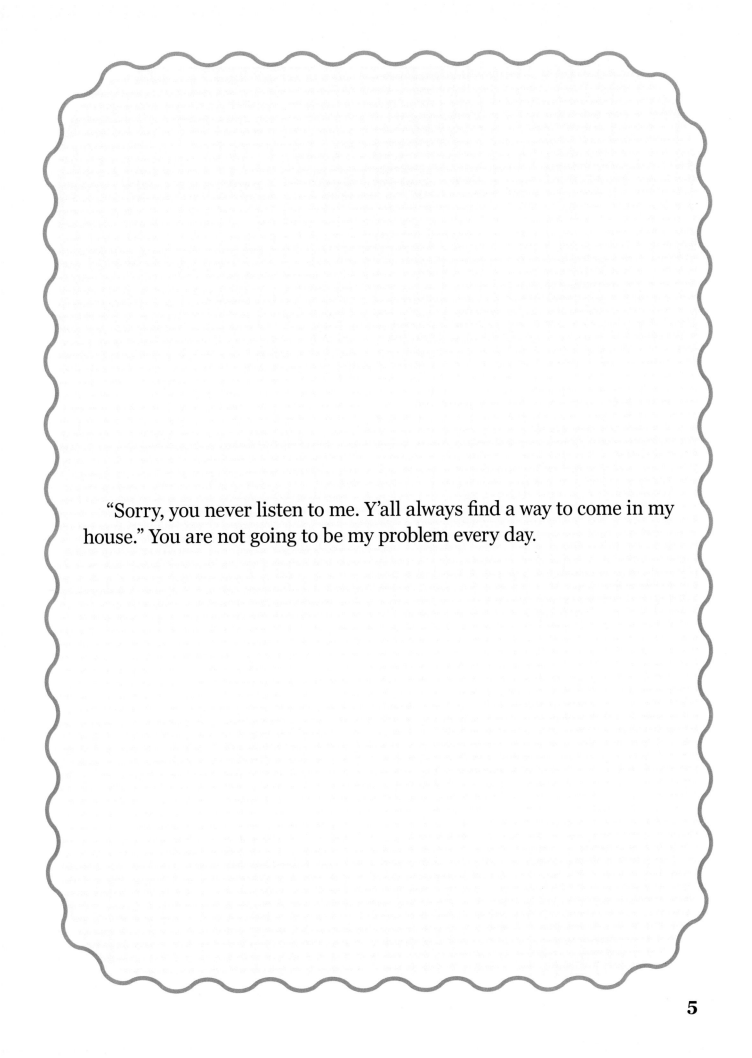

"Sorry, you never listen to me. Y'all always find a way to come in my house." You are not going to be my problem every day.

I got to run. This lady is crazy. She wants to flush me down. Let me hide. She is cruel. I saw these big giant feet after me. This lady is crazy. She is trying to kill me. I ran as fast as I could.

"You better come back here!"

No, I am scared. I have never seen a foot that big.

"Where are you? I just saw you. There you are! Gotcha! Darn it, you got away again."

Oh my! She is really scary.

I got to hide in the drawer.

"Ohhh, you are in my drawer. There you are! When I catch you, you are going to be sorry."

I am going to stay right here, under her lipstick tube. She is still here. I hear her breathing. I got to stay still, before she sees me.

"Where are you? I know you are here."

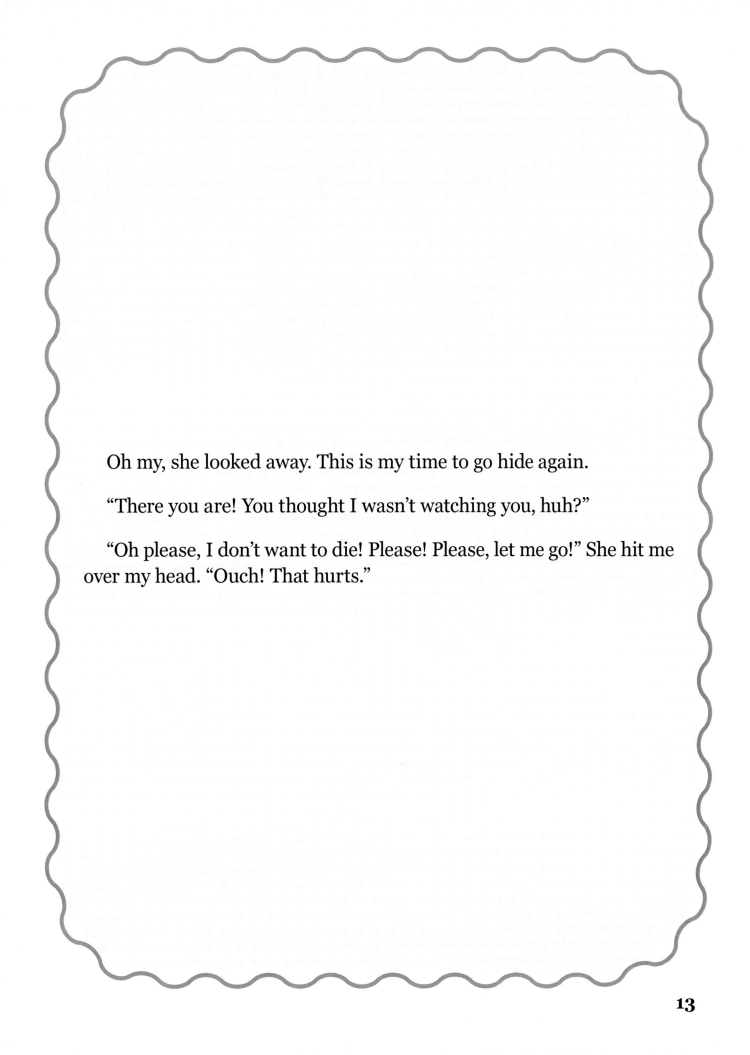

Oh my, she looked away. This is my time to go hide again.

"There you are! You thought I wasn't watching you, huh?"

"Oh please, I don't want to die! Please! Please, let me go!" She hit me over my head. "Ouch! That hurts."

"Get back here, you little creature. I am tired of you in my house. Where are you? OK, you're hiding again. You are about to make me mad at you! I am tired of you bringing germs in my house. You come in here to roll over and die. And I am the one who has to sweep up, pick up, and toss you down the toilet. You add more work to my daily schedule, and I am tired."

I got to be as quiet as possible. This lady is on a rampage trying to find me. She is really after me. What did I do so wrong? She can't stay in this big house all by herself. I only wanted to get out of the cold. My legs couldn't move outside, but the minute I walked on her hard-wood floors my legs came back to life. But if I knew I was going to be running for my life, I would have just stayed in the cold. She is about to give me an attack, or I'm about give her one while she's looking for me. You would think she has other big fish to fry, but she is really focused on finding me.

I better get the daylights out of here, I thought. But just when I thought I had the chance of my life, I could hear her walking down the hallway. Darn it, what am I going to do now? This is a long hallway. Before I could find my way back out the door, I could hear her footsteps. I thought to myself, *This lady is trying to kill me.*

"Where did he go? I know you are still here." Thinking to herself, *I know what I will do, I am going to trick him and turn off everything in the house. I will start with the radio, and then I will turn off the TV.*

Oh, I can't forget the refrigerator because that thing makes too much noise. I know I have to turn it off because if I don't he will have a chance to get away. And last, but not least, the lights were my final straw. Once I thought about turning the lights off, I stopped by the candy bowl, knowing this would be the only other sound he heard.

Oh, before she turns off the lights, this will be my chance to get away. If I don't get away now, she may find me. Down the hall I went. I was gone. I felt a sigh of relief for a change. At this time, the lights went out, and I couldn't see anything.

I ran and I ran. I am gone now from that big-foot creature. As I ran around the corner, I stumbled over something. Not knowing what I would run into once I turned the corner, I heard the scream of this loud old lady. I mean, just when I thought about getting away, this lady hollered so loud and scared the cramps out of me.

"Yuck, you ran on my feet. Just when I stopped for a break to feed my face, you run across my feet. My candy goes in the air and the paper falls onto the floor," said the lady.

I got to get away before this crazy lady turns the lights on. She won't find me this time. It's dark. This is my time to get away now. I eased down the hallway, headed to the bathroom, and I was gone.

I thought to myself, *Yay! She won't catch me now … my life is saved.* Just as I was too happy, I stepped on the darn candy paper. Man, just when I felt my life was saved, in the same sentence I knew it was over as well."

"I hear something," said the lady. "Oh, sounds like the candy wrapper he made me drop, Oh yeah, that's what it was." I immediately flipped the light on. And he was running as fast as he could. "You won't get away from these big feet." As he stepped ten feet, I stepped one foot. I was on to him. He won't get away this time. "Come back here, you little creature. You thought you had gotten away. Umhum. What the devil meant for My bad, God worked it out for my good. Although I didn't get a chance to eat my candy with you stepping on the wrapper. Help me to find your little butt."

Oh my, here she is now. I have time to think of what I had done wrong. She stepped on me, picked me up, and I knew she was really mad at me for the third or fourth time. As she was carrying me, I thought to myself, *The actions that caused her to react. First, I came in her house and scared her. I ran her on a wild bug chase throughout her house. I ran across her feet. I made her drop her candy, and the rest is history.* After she picked me up by my stomach, she smashed me, and squeezed the guts out of me.

"I was thinking to myself, *This lady is really crazy.* But I knew in order to save my life I couldn't do any more wrong. Although she was squeezing me hard, I couldn't do anything else but hold my breath because down the toilet I went.

"Take that you little creature! Don't ever come back in my house."

"I told you, I can't swim."

"I don't care, you bug me"

"You're mean, old lady. Oh, I forgot to tell you, I had my babies behind the refrigerator. You will see them when you plug it back up. Good luck catchin' them."

"Darn it."

Printed in the United States
by Baker & Taylor Publisher Services